A Child of 1971: A Tale of War, Language, and Liberation
Based on a True Story
By: Sajid Fahmid

To my grandma Jabun "Mita" Nahar Begum and my mother Rownak Jahan Huma
For sharing a war story that would otherwise be forgotten

The Fragile Silence

In the tiny room that Mita called her own, the thick curtains rustled softly. Moonlight filtered in from the Dhakaian styled windows, casting shadows that danced to the rhythms of the wind. She sat cross-legged, her fingers fidgeting, entwined with the frayed ends of her saree.

The Voice from Afar

The radio, a relic of simpler times, hummed to life. It was an old companion, connecting their home to the world beyond. Tonight, the voice that echoed from its speakers sounded distant and unfamiliar, painting pictures of tempestuous seas and nature's wrath.

Eclipsed Emotions

The year was 1970. A cyclone, the voice said. A fierce storm that had swept the coast, leaving destruction in its wake. Mita imagined the waves, monstrous and unforgiving, claiming everything in their path down in Bhola. She was safe in her home in Dhaka, but the rain only got louder outside. The very thought sent shivers down her spine, making her clutch her shawl tighter.

Lost in Thought

The water, she remembered, was a
place of joy. As a child, she had
danced along the shores with her
brother, their laughter mixing with the
song of the waves. The idea that the
same waves could now be harbingers
of death was a chilling revelation.

A Whisper in the Night

As the voice on the radio continued,
speaking of lost homes and shattered
lives from what would come to be
known as the Bhola Cyclone, she felt a
tug at her heartstrings. The weight of
the tragedy felt almost tangible,
pressing down on her chest. Mita
wondered about the countless stories,
the dreams swallowed whole by the
tempest.

Flicker of Hope

Yet, amidst the tales of devastation,
there were also stories of resilience.
Fishermen who braved the storm,
communities that came together to
rebuild. In those moments, she found
hope, a testament to the indomitable
human spirit.

Reflection

The radio fell silent, but her mind was ablaze. With every crashing wave, she felt the mingling of sorrow and hope, the intertwining dance of despair and determination. The night may have been marred by tragedy, but in its depth, Mita found the resilience to face a new dawn.

Whispers of Dhaka

Dhaka was a city of contrasts. Skyscrapers kissed the heavens, while narrow alleyways whispered tales of ancient legacies. The azan from a nearby mosque intertwined with temple bells, creating a symphony of faiths. The very air she breathed was infused with history, dreams, and the unmistakable aroma of street food.

Glimpses from the Balcony

From the intricately carved wooden balcony of their ancestral home, she often gazed at the world below. The rickshaw pullers, with their vibrant tapestries depicting scenes of pastoral beauty, the children with kites that soared higher than one's dreams, and the familiar hum of the bustling marketplace; Dhaka was alive, ever-vibrant.

A City Unaware

But tonight, Dhaka felt different. Oblivious to the distant cyclone's fury, its heartbeats seemed muffled. Mita could feel a collective sigh, as if the city, in its wisdom, anticipated a change on the horizon.

Foreshadowing of a Storm

While the cyclone had physically swept through coastal lands, its aftershocks echoed across political landscapes. West Pakistan's lack of adequate relief, their blatant indifference, was a wound that festered. Each day, the radio brought tales of sorrow, of homes lost and families torn apart. With each story, the chasm between the east and the west yawned wider.

Stirrings of a Dream

Mita remembered conversations, hushed whispers among the elders, about how West Pakistan saw them. Were they merely a colony to be milked dry? But the cyclone's aftermath had sown the seeds of a dream. A dream of autonomy, of self-governance, of a nation that could hold its head high.

The Dance of the Fireflies

In the twilight, she noticed fireflies beginning their nocturnal dance. Their gentle glow, a beacon in the dark, reminded her of hope. She didn't know it then, but they were a harbinger of a new dawn. The cyclone was not just nature's fury; it was a prelude, a catalyst for a revolution that would reshape her world, leading her people towards a taste of newfound freedom.

Awakening

The dawn of 1970 was not just the beginning of a new year, but a harbinger of the seismic shifts that awaited the nation. Dhaka, with its bustling streets and vibrant energy, could sense the stirrings of change.

Ballots and Hopes

Election booths saw unprecedented queues. People from all walks of life, young and old, rich and poor, cast their votes with fervent hope. This was not just an election; it was a collective yearning for a different future.

Awami's Rise

The results were staggering. The Awami League, under the charismatic leadership of Sheikh Mujibur Rahman, secured a landslide victory. Their promises of autonomy and a better life for the Bengali people had resonated deeply.

The West's Discontent

However, their victory was met with cold apprehension in West Pakistan. The very idea that the eastern wing, with its distinct language and culture, held the majority was unthinkable. The reluctance to transfer power was palpable.

An Omen in the Air

Whispers filled the streets of Dhaka. People spoke of the significance of this election, seeing it as an affirmation of their distinct identity. They hoped it would pave the way for greater autonomy and recognition.

Six Points and Dreams

Sheikh Mujib's "Six Points" became the talk of the town. It was a clear vision of what East Pakistan aspired for — economic freedom, a fair share of military positions, and more. It was

a blueprint for a more just and
equitable nation.

The Unyielding Gale

But as the winds of change blew
stronger, resistance from the West
grew. The monumental election had
set the stage, but the road to realizing
the dream of autonomy was fraught
with challenges.

Anticipation's Glow

Every evening, as the sun set over
Dhaka, people gathered to discuss the
day's events. The election had ignited a
spark, a fervent hope for a nation
where they could carve out their
destiny. The anticipation of what lay
ahead was both exhilarating and
daunting.

Echoes of Youth

Amidst the alleyways of Dhaka, where
children once played without care, the
weight of change felt palpable. For a
15-year-old girl, the transformation
was overwhelming. Every
conversation, every whisper, spoke of
a world much larger than her
immediate reality.

A Diary's Page

In the quiet confines of her room,
Mita scribbled furiously into her diary.
It wasn't just a record of daily events
but a canvas of her emotions — the
exhilaration, the confusion, the
nascent hope.

Classroom Whispers

In school, hushed conversations
replaced regular chatter. The election
was not just a political event; it was a
symbol of change, a topic of debate
even among the youngest. She, too,
found herself drawn into discussions,
her opinions evolving with each
passing day.

Family Gatherings

Evenings at home were filled with
animated discussions. Her older
brother, always a political enthusiast,
passionately spoke of Sheikh Mujib's
vision. Her heart swelled with pride,
but also ached with an undefined
worry for her brother, who seemed
increasingly drawn to the political
fervor.

Dreams and Desires

Every night, as Mita lay on her bed, staring at the dimly lit ceiling, she dreamt. Dreams not just of personal aspirations, but of a nation on the cusp of transformation. She imagined a future where she could voice her thoughts without fear, where her identity as a Bengali and a woman was celebrated.

Amidst Uncertainty

The hesitance of the West was no secret. Conversations at home often revolved around it. The fear of the unknown loomed large. She felt it too — a mix of excitement for what lay ahead and trepidation for the challenges it brought.

Bridging Two Worlds

Being young in such tumultuous times was a double-edged sword. She grappled with her own adolescent challenges while trying to make sense of the political whirlwind around her. Yet, this period also shaped her, molding her into a young woman acutely aware of her surroundings and her place within it.

The Glimmering Horizon

As days turned to nights and nights to days, one thing remained unchanged — her unwavering hope. The hope that the winds of change would usher in a new dawn, not just for the nation but for the young girl who dreamt of freedom, in every sense of the word.

Streets Ablaze

Dhaka's streets, once filled with the everyday cacophony, now echoed a different tune. Protests, rallies, passionate speeches – the city was a hive of activity. From her window, she watched the waves of people, their chants forming a rhythmic beat that pulsed through the heart of the city.

Innocence and Rebellion

Her once simple schoolyard was transformed. No longer just a place for games and laughter, it became a space for discussions, debates, and the occasional planning of a rally. Her friends, with whom Mita once shared innocent tales, now exchanged whispered news of the latest protest.

Yearning to Participate

She felt an inner turmoil. The adolescent desire to be a part of something bigger, to join the masses on the streets, clashed with the protective cocoon her family had built around her. She yearned to raise her voice, to be heard amidst the clamor.

The Arrest

The day's events were a blur. News of Mujibur Rahman's arrest spread like wildfire. Her heart raced, thoughts of her own brother at the forefront. The very air seemed charged with tension, as emotions of anger, fear, and defiance mingled.

Veiled Defiance

Every evening, the women in her neighborhood gathered, their voices a melodic blend of sorrow and hope. They sang of their land, their rights, their desires. In their songs, she felt a veiled defiance, an assertion of identity amidst the surrounding chaos.

Hidden Desires

In the quiet of her room, Mita penned down her thoughts, dreams, and fears. The diary was a refuge, a place to pour out her desires. Desires for a free nation, for her voice to matter, and for the safety of her family, especially her brother, whose fervent involvement worried her.

The Weight of Youth

Growing up amidst such fervor was no easy task. Balancing the responsibilities of school, the allure of the protests, and the constant worry for her family became her daily life. She was at the crossroads, teetering between the innocence of youth and the weight of the times.

A Tapestry of Emotions

Each day brought with it a rollercoaster of emotions. Joy at the unity she saw around her, sorrow at the escalating tensions, and a burning desire to play her part. As Dhaka stood on the precipice of monumental change, so too did the young girl, ready to embrace her destiny.

Whispers of Operation

Rumors began to circulate. Hushed conversations in the bazaars, panicked whispers in the alleyways – talks of an impending military crackdown. As Dhaka's streets brimmed with anticipation, she felt the knot of anxiety tighten in her stomach.

Emissaries from the West

With rising tensions, emissaries from
West Pakistan were sent to the east in
an attempt to negotiate. But their
efforts often felt insincere, only
stoking the flames of mistrust. Mita
overheard her father's heated
discussions, speaking of the deceit and
the games of the West.

The Evening Curfew

The sunsets brought unease. As
darkness descended, so did the
curfews. The once lively streets of
Dhaka silenced, replaced by the
footsteps of patrolling soldiers. Staring
into the night, she would imagine a
different world, one free from the
shadows of oppression.

The Resilience of Youth

Yet, even in these daunting times, the
resilience of youth shone through.
makeshift cricket games in the alleys,
the clandestine exchanges of
revolutionary literature in school – life
tried to push forward. For her, it was a
blend of typical teenage rebellion and
a deeper longing for freedom.

Echoes of Lahore

News from the western wing trickled in. Talks of the famous Lahore Resolution of years past, the initial calls for a separate state. A stark reminder that dreams could be realized, but not without sacrifices. She pondered, was East Pakistan destined for a similar fate?

Clashes and Casualties

Each day brought reports of fresh skirmishes. Students against the army, civilians against the state. With each casualty, her resolve hardened. The pain was personal; every lost life felt like a brother, a friend, a part of her very soul.

University Ground Zero

Dhaka University became ground zero. A hub for intellectual debate, now a symbol of resistance. She'd hear tales of brave students, standing their ground, their spirits unbroken despite the odds. Their stories became her nightly lullabies, tales of courage in the face of adversity.

A Sister's Fear

But amidst the admiration lay fear. Every rally her brother attended, every protest he spoke at, Mita feared it might be his last. Each time he stepped out, she would grip the end of her saree, silently praying for his safe return, while battling the urge to join him in his fight.

The Tapestry Unravels

Dhaka, a city of rich history and vibrant culture, was on the brink. The intricate tapestry of its people, their dreams and struggles, was beginning to unravel. And at its heart, a young girl, caught in the whirlwind, stood resilient, a symbol of hope for a brighter tomorrow.

Darkening Skies

The vibrant hues of Dhaka's sky began to cloud over, reflecting the mood of its inhabitants. A sense of foreboding hung heavy, as if nature itself was bracing for the impending tempest. She felt it too, an unsettling quiet before the storm.

Grim News Broadcasts

Every radio brought tidings of unease. Statements from the West, defiant speeches from local leaders, and ever-growing reports of military movements. Huddled with her family, each broadcast heightened their collective anxiety.

Militant Movements

From her balcony, she observed increased patrols, convoys of army vehicles, and unfamiliar faces. Whispers of "Operation Searchlight" made rounds, though its full implications remained shrouded in mystery.

Symbols of Hope

Yet, in these darkening times, symbols of hope persisted. The golden fish of her flag, the melody of "Amar Sonar Bangla", and tales of past heroes – they became beacons, reminding her of the indomitable Bengali spirit.

Streets of Caution

Walking the streets of Dhaka became an exercise in caution. Soldiers at checkpoints, scrutinizing eyes, and the constant murmur of unrest. With every step, she felt the gravity of the times, the weight of a storm brewing.

Silent Preparations

At home, preparations were made in hushed tones. Stockpiling essentials, creating safe spaces, and rehearsing emergency protocols. The once joyful household was now a fortress, bracing for the unknown.

A Brother's Oath

Late one night, she overheard her brother, a fervent promise to defend their motherland. His voice, tinged with passion and fear, made her heart wretch. She knew the storm would demand sacrifices, and she silently prayed her family wouldn't pay its heavy price.

City on Edge

Dhaka, the heart of East Pakistan, throbbed with tension. A city on edge, waiting, watching, and hoping. As the storm clouds gathered, so did her resolve, for she knew that the impending tempest would reshape her world forever.

Sinister Silence

The dusk settled with an eerie calmness. The usual cacophony of Dhaka's nightlife is replaced by a stifling silence. As darkness deepened, so did the sense of foreboding in her

heart. Mita clutched her diary close,
every beat of her heart echoing the
city's tense anticipation.

First Shots Fired

The suddenness of it was jarring.
Gunfire erupted, distant but
unmistakable. The abstract fear that
had loomed became a tangible terror.
Every shot seemed to pierce the
protective bubble of her childhood,
thrusting her into a nightmarish
reality.

Echoes from the University

Distant flames illuminated the
horizon, painting a fiery silhouette of
Dhaka University. Stories had warned
of its targeting, and tonight, those
fears came alive. From her vantage, it
was a beacon of both defiance and
despair.

Huddled Together

Family became a sanctuary. Huddled
together, their collective warmth was
both literal and emotional. Prayers
whispered, comforting embraces
shared, and promises of protection
exchanged. In that room, she felt the
weight of love and the burden of
impending separation.

Gone Communications

The radio, their link to the outside world, went eerily silent. Static replaced news, amplifying the isolation. Each attempt to tune in only intensified the realization: Dhaka was cut off, and they were alone amidst the chaos.

Whispers of Escape

Between the gunfire, hurried discussions of escape routes and safe havens emerged. Neighbors whispered of the countryside, of relatives in distant villages, and of paths less patrolled. But for her, the thought of leaving her beloved Dhaka was a heartbreak in itself.

A Solemn Vow

Amidst the terror, a moment of clarity crystallized. Gazing at her reflection, dimly lit by the candle's flicker, Mita made a silent pledge. No matter the storm's aftermath, she would stand resilient, preserving the stories, the pain, and the hope of this fateful night.

Dawn's First Light

As dawn approached, the sounds of battle persisted but were now accompanied by the chirping of the city's early birds. A symbolic juxtaposition of nature's hope and man's destruction. With the rising sun, she braced herself to face the aftermath of the night of fire, a world irrevocably changed.

News of Brutality

Each morning, harrowing tales reached her ears. Stories of indiscriminate firing, burned villages, and silenced voices. Operation Searchlight was no longer just a whispered term; it was a living nightmare unfolding before Dhaka's very eyes.

Brother's Farewell

The decision was abrupt but inevitable. Her brother, with resolve in his eyes and fire in his heart, chose to defend their homeland. Their farewell, a mix of pride and despair, was a moment etched in her memory. His whispered promise to return was a beacon she'd hold onto in the days to come.

The Empty Chair

Every meal was a stark reminder. His
empty chair, a symbol of his absence.
The silence at the dinner table was
loud, deafening, each bite a struggle as
memories of happier times played in
her mind.

Sleepless Nights

Nights were the hardest. Tossing and
turning, she'd relive their childhood
memories. The playful banters, shared
dreams, and protective embraces.
Each night, she'd send a silent prayer
skyward, willing him to stay safe
amidst the chaos.

Letters from the Front

Occasionally, a scribbled note would
arrive. His hurried handwriting spoke
of battles, camaraderie, and the
unyielding spirit of the Mukti Bahini.
While his words tried to reassure, the
underlying tone betrayed the
harshness of his reality.

Echoes of Valor

From whispered conversations, she
learned of her brother's bravery.
Stories of his leadership, his courage
under fire, and his relentless drive to

push back the oppressors. Each tale, a mix of pride and fear, solidified his place as her hero.

An Unyielding Hope

With each passing day, her hope grew stronger. Clinging to every positive story, every victory, and every moment of respite, she willed the universe to protect him. Every sunrise was a testament to her undying hope, and every sunset, a promise of a brighter tomorrow.

The Inescapable Reality

But amidst the hope, the reality of war weighed heavily. She knew that with every victory came losses, with every triumphant tale, there were untold stories of pain. As Operation Searchlight raged on, she navigated the torturous limbo between hope and the dread of the unknown.

City's Scars

Dhaka bore witness to the brutality. Burned houses, deserted streets, and graffiti-covered walls telling tales of defiance. As she wandered the alleys, every mark became a chronicle of her city's pain and resilience.

Tales from Refugees

Families streamed into Dhaka, fleeing
the countryside's horror. Their sunken
eyes and broken spirits told stories
even before they spoke. Each tale
added layers to her understanding,
painting a bleak picture of the
Operation's vast reach.

Glimpses in Photographs

Occasionally, newspapers would carry
photographs of the warfront. Each
time, her eyes would frantically search
for a familiar face, for any sign of her
brother amidst the smoke and rubble.
Those images, both haunting and
hopeful, became her windows to his
world.

Songs of Resistance

Music became a refuge. Melodies of
resistance, lyrics of hope, and rhythms
of rebellion echoed in every corner of
the city. They were reminders that the
spirit of Bangladesh remained
unbroken, and Mita found solace in
their comforting embrace.

Unsettling Quiet

There were days when an unsettling quiet would grip the city. The silence, a heavy cloak, hinted at an impending storm or a brief respite. In those moments, she'd find herself holding her breath, waiting for the next chapter of their tumultuous journey.

Dreams and Nightmares

Sleep was a double-edged sword. Dreams where her brother returned, victorious and unscarred, were often chased away by nightmares of loss and despair. Waking up became a daily confrontation with reality, a mix of relief and longing.

Moments of Defiance

Amid the gloom, moments of defiance shone bright. Women rallying together, children distributing clandestine leaflets, and the elderly sharing tales of past struggles. Their collective resistance was a testament to Dhaka's indomitable spirit.

The Weight of Waiting

Days turned into weeks, and weeks into months. The calendar pages became a testament to her wait, each day marked with hope and anxiety. As Operation Searchlight raged on, she

anchored herself in memories, prayers,
and the unwavering belief that they'd
reunite in a free Bangladesh.

The Dreaded Knock

It came without warning. A knock,
hesitant but firm, followed by hushed
voices. The bearer of the news, a
comrade of her brother, looked as
shattered as the message he carried.
Her world spun as she heard the
words: her brother was no more.

Tears of Disbelief

The tears came unbidden, each
droplet a testament to her anguish.
But amidst the sorrow was a strong
undercurrent of disbelief. Her heart
refused to accept, to comprehend, that
her beacon of hope had been
extinguished.

A Plea to the Masses

Determined, she took to the airwaves.
Crafting a heartfelt plea, detailing her
brother's features, recounting their last
conversation. As her voice echoed
through countless homes, it was a mix
of desperation, hope, and love.

Responses Pour In

The city responded. Phone calls, letters, and strangers at the doorstep. Each bringing tales, sightings, and narratives. Some shared stories of their own lost loved ones, creating a tapestry of collective grief and shared hope.

Visits to the Unknown

Guided by these tales, she visited makeshift camps, hospitals, and shelters. Her eyes, always searching, hoping to catch a glimpse of a familiar face. Each visit was a rollercoaster of emotions, a dance between hope and heartbreak.

The Weight of Reality

With each passing day and each unfruitful lead, the weight of reality bore down on her. The optimism that had initially fueled her search began to waver, replaced by a creeping despair.

A Nation's Embrace

Yet, in her darkest moments, the nation embraced her. Letters of comfort, songs dedicated to her quest, and countless prayers. Her personal tragedy had become emblematic of

Bangladesh's collective sorrow, and in this shared grief, she found strength.

Acceptance and Resolve

Slowly, the shadows began to lift. Though her heart was heavy with loss, it was also filled with determination. She would continue her brother's legacy, ensuring that his dreams for a free Bangladesh would live on. Her search might have ended, but her journey was just beginning.

Memories Preserved

Within her room, she built a shrine of memories. Photos, letters, and mementos. Each object has a tangible connection to her brother. In those quiet moments, surrounded by remnants of the past, Mita felt his presence, guiding and comforting her.

Ripples in the Community

Word of her quest spread far and wide. People from distant towns reached out, sharing their stories, extending their empathy. Her brother's tale became a beacon, a symbol of the countless unsung heroes of the liberation war.

Echoes of Yesterday

Walking through the streets of Dhaka, every corner whispered tales of her brother. The playgrounds they raced through, the mango tree under which they shared secrets, and the rooftops where they dreamt of the future. These echoes of yesterday kept her connection with him alive.

Stories from the Frontlines

Veterans of the war approached her, sharing tales of her brother's valor. Of battles fought side by side, of nights spent under starry skies sharing dreams of freedom. Each story, a bittersweet mix of pride and pain, further painted the portrait of her brother's legacy.

The Silver Lining

With the darkness of loss came a newfound purpose. She became a pillar of strength for others, counseling families, sharing her coping mechanisms, and becoming a beacon of hope for those navigating their grief.

A Dream Rekindled

One evening, watching the sun set over Dhaka, she felt a renewed sense of purpose. Inspired by her brother's dreams and fueled by the nation's spirit, she decided to take up the mantle of resistance. Her path was clear: she would join the Mukti Bahini.

Ties That Bind

The community rallied around her decision. Some offered training, others words of encouragement. As she prepared for this new chapter, she felt the collective embrace of her city, her nation, all propelling her forward in her mission.

Closing the Chapter

As the days turned into nights, she began to find closure. The radio announcement, the countless searches, and the tales of her brother had all led her to this moment. With a heavy heart but an unyielding spirit, she was ready to write the next chapter of her life, carrying her brother's legacy forward in the quest for a free Bangladesh.

Awakening Fire

The void left by her brother's absence transformed into an insatiable fire within her. No longer just the little sister who waited, she emerged as a young woman, determined to be the change, to take the fight to the frontlines.

Training Days

Mornings were grueling, filled with drills and lessons. Mud-streaked face, sweat-soaked clothes, yet her spirit never wavered. Each bruise, a badge of honor. Every drop of sweat, a testament to her dedication.

Whispers of Doubt

Not everyone understood. Murmurs in the community questioned her place in the Mukti Bahini. "A girl? In the war?" they'd whisper. But every doubt only strengthened her resolve.

Lessons in Courage

Veteran fighters became her mentors. Through them, she learned not just the techniques of warfare but the ethos of the Mukti Bahini. Their stories of resilience and courage fueled her journey.

Moment of Truth

The day arrived when her training was put to the test. Facing the enemy, she channeled her grief, her love for her brother, and her dream of a free Bangladesh. Each move, each decision, reflected her unwavering commitment.

A Legacy Carried Forward

On the battlefield, she wasn't just fighting for her country; she was upholding her brother's legacy. With every strategic move, every saved comrade, Mita felt his spirit guiding her.

The Weight of Leadership

As days turned into weeks, she found herself taking on leadership roles. Guiding younger fighters, planning strategic attacks, and making difficult decisions. The once sheltered girl from Dhaka had grown into a formidable force.

The Bonds of Brotherhood

Her fellow Mukti Bahini fighters became her new family. Together, they shared meals, stories, and dreams. The camaraderie built on the battlefield

transcended gender, age, and
background.

Embracing Dual Identities

At camp, she'd often reflect on her
journey. From a hopeful sister waiting
for her brother's return to a warrior
on the frontlines. Embracing these
dual identities, she realized, was her
strength. She wasn't just fighting as a
Mukti Bahini member; she was
fighting as a sister, carrying the weight
of her brother's dreams and the hopes
of her nation.

Echos in the Silence

Nights at the camp were often filled
with an eerie silence, broken only by
distant gunshots or the soft rustling of
leaves. Lying on her makeshift bed,
she'd replay memories of her brother,
drawing strength from their shared
dreams.

Challenges Beyond Combat

The war wasn't just about fighting the
enemy. It was about navigating the
challenges that came with it: rationing
food, tending to the wounded, and
boosting the morale of her fellow
soldiers. Each challenge met, she grew
not just as a fighter, but as a leader.

Inspirations in Ink

In quiet moments, she'd pen down her experiences, capturing the essence of the war, her feelings, her challenges, and her hopes. These writings would later inspire countless others, serving as a testament to her journey.

Facing Losses

The grim reality of war became evident with each fallen comrade. Mourning their loss, she'd remember her brother, understanding the grief of countless families back home. But with each loss, her resolve only solidified further.

Symbols and Memories

Around her neck, she wore her brother's old pendant. It had been his lucky charm, and now it was hers. Touching it before every mission, she felt a connection, a silent promise between the siblings.

Women of the War

Mita wasn't alone. Other women, driven by their own stories, joined the fight. Together, they shattered stereotypes, proving that bravery and patriotism knew no gender. Their tales of valor would become legends in the annals of Bangladesh's history.

Dreams of Tomorrow

As the battles raged on, she allowed herself to dream of a future beyond the war. A free Bangladesh, where stories like hers would inspire generations. Where her brother's memory would live on, not just as a tale of loss, but as a beacon of hope and determination.

The Final Stand

As the days of the liberation war began to wane, she stood tall, ready for the final push. Armed with memories, driven by purpose, and fueled by the collective spirit of her nation, she was prepared to give it her all, ensuring her brother's dream of a free Bangladesh became a reality.

Whispers of Victory

Word began to spread throughout the camps: the enemy was weakening, victory was on the horizon. As hope surged, she could almost hear the jubilant cries of her people, echoing

the dreams of freedom she and her
brother once shared.

The Armor of Faith

As the days grew more perilous, her
reliance on faith deepened. In the
quiet moments before dawn, she'd
offer prayers, seeking protection for
her comrades and strength for the
battles ahead. It was this faith that
became her shield, guarding her spirit
amidst the chaos.

Echoes of Home

Every letter she received from home
was a balm to her weary heart.
Reading words of pride from her
parents, updates about her
neighborhood in Dhaka, and the
undying belief that they'd soon be
reunited, fueled her drive.

The Weight of Decisions

With her growing responsibilities, the
decisions became tougher. Planning
ambushes, rescuing captured
comrades, and rationing dwindling
supplies. Each choice carried weight,
but she made them with a clarity of
purpose, knowing she was upholding
her brother's legacy.

Tales around the Fire

At night, huddled around campfires, stories were exchanged. Tales of heroism, love, loss, and hope. She'd often share anecdotes of her brother, and in return, hear stories of others, weaving a rich tapestry of shared experiences.

The Final Letter

One evening, she penned what she believed might be her last letter home. Filled with love, hope, and a promise to meet again, either in this life or the next. Sealing it with a tear and a prayer, she entrusted it to a comrade heading to Dhaka.

The Dawn of a New Day

As the first rays of sun pierced the horizon, signaling what many believed would be the final battle, Mita took a deep breath. Clutching her brother's pendant, memories of their shared dreams played in her mind. She knew she wasn't just fighting for freedom; she was fighting for the promise of a brighter tomorrow for all of Bangladesh.

A Moment Suspended

In the heat of the battle, time seemed
to stand still. Each explosion, every
cry, felt like an eternity. Yet, amidst the
chaos, she moved with a fierce
determination, a dance of resistance
and hope, echoing her unwavering
resolve.

Silent Rebellion

As she walked through the camp, she
could feel the weight of countless
gazes upon her. Some filled with
admiration, others with doubt. Yet,
with every step, she became a symbol.
A testament to every woman who
dared to defy societal expectations.

Warrior in a Sari

One day, draped in a traditional sari,
she took to the training grounds.
Demonstrating that her choice of
attire didn't diminish her skill or
determination. She wasn't just a
soldier; she was a beacon of tradition
and change, intertwined.

Voices of the Unheard

She wasn't the only one. All around,
women were rising, each with their
own story, their own fury. They were

the mothers who had lost children, the
sisters waiting for brothers, the
daughters of a nation on the brink.
Their collective roar was deafening.

Beyond the Battlefield

Her fight wasn't just against the
external enemy. It was against the
internal prejudices that sought to
define her place. Every time she
bandages a wound or strategizes an
attack, she shatters yet another
stereotype.

Conversations in the Shadows

Late at night, she'd join hushed
gatherings of women. Sharing stories,
they'd draw strength from one
another. These were the unsung
heroes, their tales often
overshadowed, but their spirit as fierce
as any.

Empowerment in Unity

Together with her fellow women
warriors, they formed a formidable
force. Their unity, a message to all:
They were not to be underestimated
or sidelined. They were the heart of
the Mukti Bahini, pumping lifeblood
into the fight for freedom.

The Gaze Returned

With every doubtful gaze Mita met,
she responded not with anger, but
with determination. Training harder,
fighting fiercer, leading with grace and
grit. Her actions, a silent retort to
every question raised about her place
in this war.

Legacy in Motion

Young girls, hearing tales of her
bravery, began to dream bigger. They
saw in her a future where they too
could lead, fight, and carve their own
paths. She was no longer just a soldier;
she was an inspiration, a spark of
feminine fury that would ignite
generations to come.

Lessons in Duality

In the stillness of dawn, she'd often
reflect on her duality. The delicate
dance between being a caring sister
and a fierce warrior. It was a balance
she embraced, understanding that her
femininity added depth to her
strength.

Whispered Songs of Revolution

Music played a pivotal role in her journey. The soft, poignant tunes of traditional Bengali songs merged with the anthems of revolution. They sang of love, loss, and liberation, their notes wrapping around her like a comforting shawl.

Challenging Expectations

Each day brought new challenges, not just from the enemy, but from within her ranks. Questions about her capabilities, murmurs about her 'place'. But with every challenge met head-on, she became a living testament to feminine prowess.

Letters of Encouragement

She'd receive notes, often scribbled in haste, from women across Bangladesh. Words of gratitude, tales of shared struggles, and pledges of solidarity. They served as reminders that her fight extended beyond the confines of the camp.

The Power of Softness

In moments of respite, she'd tend to the injured, her gentle touch a stark contrast to her warrior spirit. It was a reminder that compassion and courage could coexist, that the softness of her femininity was an asset, not a weakness.

The Grit Behind the Grace

While many saw her grace, few recognized the grit that powered her every move. The countless hours of training, the sleepless nights, the personal sacrifices - all were masked by her poised demeanor.

Dreams of a New Dawn

As the days wore on, she dreamt of a Bangladesh where stories like hers were not the exception but the norm. A nation where young girls grew up hearing tales of valiant women, where they were encouraged to dream without boundaries.

A Dance of Defiance

One evening, as the sun set, casting a golden hue over the camp, she danced. It was a dance of defiance, of joy, of sorrow. A dance that encapsulated her journey, resonating with the rhythmic heartbeat of a nation on the brink of rebirth. Her movement, an embodiment of the feminine fury that fueled the fight for freedom.

Arrival of the Allies

With December came a shift in the wind. The arrival of the Indian forces signaled a turning point in the war. Their presence, formidable and unwavering, bolstered the spirits of the Mukti Bahini and civilians alike. Dhaka, once a city of despair, buzzed with cautious optimism.

Tales of Unity

As battles raged on, stories began to emerge of unparalleled cooperation between the Bengali fighters and their Indian counterparts. In trenches and on warfronts, languages and borders blurred, replaced by a shared goal of liberation.

The Weight of Sacrifice

The closer they got to victory, the more palpable the cost became. Every street bore scars, every home a tale of loss. Amidst the chaos, Mita found herself returning to memories of her brother, the driving force behind her journey.

Countdown to Freedom

As December 16th neared, the intensity of the struggle grew. Every dawn brought them closer to their dream, every sunset a reminder of the trials they'd endured. The air was thick with anticipation, hope, and the collective prayers of millions.

Victory Day Dawns

And then it came - December 16th. The day the sun rose on a free Bangladesh. Jubilant cries echoed through the streets, the tricolor flag of Bangladesh flapping proudly in the breeze. It was a moment frozen in time, the culmination of months of struggle, sacrifice, and resilience.

Rebuilding Amidst Ruins

In the days that followed, the true extent of the devastation became clear. Dhaka, once a thriving city, lay in ruins. Yet, amidst the rubble, there was a determination to rebuild, to rise from the ashes, stronger and united.

A Sister's Tribute

She returned to her family home, the weight of her brother's absence heavier than ever. In his memory, she erected a small monument, inscribing his name and the date he left for war.

It stood as a testament to his bravery
and the countless others who'd given
their lives for freedom.

Carrying the Torch Forward

The war might have ended, but her
journey was far from over. With the
birth of the new nation, she embraced
a new role - that of a guardian,
ensuring that the sacrifices made were
never forgotten. Her story, and that of
countless others, would be passed
down, a reminder of the price of
freedom and the indomitable spirit of
Bangladesh.

Echoes of War

Every corner of Dhaka whispered
tales of bravery, of heartache, of
relentless struggle. Buildings bore the
scars of battles fought, but also
became canvases for murals and art,
celebrating the spirit of the newly free
nation.

Mingled Joy and Grief

While the streets erupted in
celebrations, private moments were
often tinged with sorrow. Families
gathered, rejoicing in reunions, yet
also mourning empty seats at dinner

tables. Victory was sweet, but it came
with the bitter realization of the cost.

New Responsibilities

As the euphoria of Victory Day
ebbed, the enormity of the task ahead
became clear. Building a new nation
required everyone's effort. She found
herself navigating the challenges of
post-war recovery, leveraging her
wartime experiences to bring about
healing and unity.

A Nation's Gratitude

December 16th became an annual day
of reflection and celebration. Parades
showcased the country's resilience,
while candlelit vigils honored the
fallen. Every year, she'd stand, a proud
beacon, embodying the nation's
gratitude for her service.

Stories Passed Down

Children, wide-eyed and eager, would
gather around her, hungry for tales
from the war. She'd recount stories,
not just of battles and strategies, but
of friendships forged, of moments of
kindness amidst the chaos, and of the
relentless hope that fueled their
journey.

A Personal Journey

The war changed her, molding her from a young girl into a formidable woman. As Mita walked the streets of Dhaka, past familiar landmarks, memories would flood back. Each location a backdrop to a chapter of her journey, each story a stitch in the tapestry of her life.

Legacy of Loss and Love

Years later, the pain of her brother's loss remained, a constant companion. Yet, it was intertwined with pride for the nation they'd both fought for. She became a living testament to the power of love, loss, and the enduring human spirit.

Towards Tomorrow

With the scars of war gradually healing, she looked towards the future. Her dreams now expanded beyond personal vendettas to encompass the prosperity of Bangladesh. Her legacy, a reminder of the sacrifices made, would inspire future generations to cherish their hard-won freedom and work towards a brighter tomorrow.

Remnants of the Past

Walking the streets of post-independence Dhaka, she felt the pull of history with every step. The remnants of West Pakistan's presence, now Pakistan, lurked in the shadows. Yet, she had learned, hatred consumed the hater, not the hated. Time had given her perspective. While the wounds were deep, she saw the importance of moving forward, not in forgetting, but in forgiving for her own peace.

Martyr's Shadow

Her brother's absence was a constant presence in her life. His bravery, his sacrifice, had elevated him to the status of a martyr – a "shahid". The Shahid Minar, standing tall and proud in Dhaka, became a place of solace for her. Beneath its pillars, she'd often reflect on her journey and the love for the Bengali language that intertwined their destinies.

Melodies of Memory

The lilting cadence of the Bengali language, a symbol of cultural pride and defiance, continued to play a vital role in her life. The same tunes they had once hummed as children, and later as symbols of resistance, now served as lullabies for her own children. The language was more than just words; it was the heartbeat of Bangladesh.

Beyond the Battle

While her role as a combatant was etched in history, her identity as a woman brought its own challenges and triumphs. Post-war, she became a beacon for countless women, proving that femininity and strength were not mutually exclusive. Mita used her influence to empower the next generation of Bengali women, ensuring they knew their worth and potential.

Shahid's Legacy

Her brother's legacy lived on, not just in stories but in tangible actions. Schools and initiatives in his name became a testament to the power of sacrifice. His spirit, she felt, continued to guide her, ensuring she never lost her way.

Unified in Diversity

While the divide with West Pakistan had resulted in heartbreak, she now championed unity in diversity within Bangladesh. Every dialect, every regional nuance, was celebrated,

highlighting the rich tapestry that
made up the nation.

Living for Tomorrow

As the years went by, her focus shifted
to ensuring a brighter future for
Bangladesh. Her wartime experiences
served as a foundation, but her vision
extended far beyond. Education,
women's rights, and cultural
preservation became her guiding stars.

A Life's Symphony

Her life had been a series of highs and
lows, battles and triumphs, losses, and
celebrations. And through it all, the
love for her brother, her country, and
her language remained unwavering.
Her story, like the melodies of
Bangladesh, would continue to inspire,
resonate, and echo for generations to
come.

A Place of Healing

Over time, her home in Dhaka
evolved into more than just a
residence. Its walls bore witness to
countless tales and became a place of
healing for many. Veterans, fellow
combatants, and even the younger
generation flocked to her, seeking
solace, guidance, or just a listening ear.

Language of the Heart

As the years passed, the significance of the Bengali language in her life only deepened. Its verses, its poetry, its songs became her refuge. She often found herself recounting tales of the 1952 Language Movement, emphasizing how the love for their language was a precursor to their quest for independence.

A Feminine Force

The societal norms had always been a challenge. But post-war, she was a testament to breaking barriers. Her legacy was not just as a combatant but as a beacon for women's empowerment. She launched initiatives to support women in various fields, ensuring that the next generation had fewer battles to fight off the battlefield.

Brother's Beacon

At the heart of her home stood a small memorial for her brother. Lit every evening, it became a beacon for many, symbolizing hope, sacrifice, and undying love. The flame, unwavering and eternal, mirrored her commitment to keeping his memory alive.

Building Bridges

Though the scars of the past with West Pakistan were undeniable, she advocated for building bridges rather than barriers. Engaging in cultural exchanges, she sought to highlight the shared history, music, and art, focusing on unity and shared human experiences.

The Annual Pilgrimage

Every year, on Victory Day, she would make her way to the Shahid Minar. Standing tall among fellow countrymen, she'd pay her respects, her heart swelling with pride and gratitude. The monument, a symbol of sacrifice for the Bengali language, was a poignant reminder of her and her brother's intertwined destinies.

Eyes on the Horizon

While she remained deeply rooted in her past, her gaze was firmly set on the future. Through educational initiatives, cultural programs, and community development, she endeavored to lay a foundation for a prosperous Bangladesh.

Echoes in Eternity

Her journey, a blend of pain,
resilience, love, and triumph, became a
part of the nation's folklore. As tales
of her valor and commitment were
passed down, Mita became an
enduring symbol of Bangladesh's spirit
at the ripe age of 15, ensuring that her,
her brother's, and the nation's
sacrifices would never fade into
oblivion.

Printed in Great Britain
by Amazon

43859319R00036